Rain, Rain, Go Away!

Water balloon–size raindrops crashed down on the kids as they stood on the far side of the river. The rain was cold and they huddled in a circle, wrapping their arms around one another to stay warm.

Principal Nosair leaned his head out a window. "We've called the Coast Guard!" he yelled. "They're sending a tugboat!"

The ground was so wet, the kids' feet sank into the mud up to their ankles.

Horace hid behind a bush and felt his backpack. It was wet on the outside, but he knew the inside would be dry. It held both his Cupcaked Crusader costume and a cupcake he could eat to give him powers.

He took a ball of foil from his backpack and unwrapped it. The cupcake was in the shape of a circus tent with red-and-white stripes and a flag on top. Would this give him enough powers to save the kids?

OTHER BOOKS YOU MAY ENJOY

THE CUPCAKED CRUSADER

The Most Evil, Friendly Villain Ever

by Lawrence David

illustrated by Barry Gott

PUFFIN BOOKS

For Amy Herskovitz

—L.D.

PUFFIN BOOKS
Published by Penguin Group
Penguin Young Readers Group,
345 Hudson Street, New York, New York 10014, U.S.A.
Penguin Books Ltd, 80 Strand, London WC2R ORL, England
Penguin Books Australia Ltd, 250 Camberwell Road, Camberwell, Victoria 3124, Australia
Penguin Books Canada Ltd, 10 Alcorn Avenue, Toronto, Ontario, Canada M4V 3B2
Penguin Books (N.Z.) Ltd, 182-190 Wairau Road, Auckland 10, New Zealand

Published simultaneously by Dutton Children's Books and Puffin Books,
divisions of Penguin Young Readers Group, 2004

1   3   5   7   9   10   8   6   4   2

Text copyright © Lawrence David, 2004
Illustrations copyright © Barry Gott, 2004

All rights reserved
CIP Data is available.

Puffin Books ISBN 0-14-240136-6
Printed in the United States of America

Contents

THE WORST RECESS EVER

The sun shone down on Blootinville Elementary, and kids all across the playground were enjoying recess.

Some kids played Celernip Toss. They held a celernip in the waist of their pants, let it roll down a leg, and then kicked the vegetable into the air.

Some kids played on the Twisted Maniac, climbing through its maze of pipes until their arms were tangled with other kids' legs.

Barumph, awwwrp, and *mrrrowbb* could be

heard coming from the mouths of kids playing on the Esophagus Eliminator. They had strapped their bodies in the swings and were bouncing right, left, up, down, forward, and backward. When the kids' screams got as loud as one thousand fire alarms, Mrs. Buttonslip, the school janitor, leaned out her office window and told the kids to hush up or she'd plunge their lungs *and* esophaguses out.

Ten-year-old Horace Splattly wandered the school yard with a frown on his face and his backpack slung over a shoulder. It just wasn't easy being the shortest kid in all of Blootinville Elementary, except for the kindergartners and six of the first graders.

Because he was only thirty inches tall, the kids playing Celernip Toss said he was too little to join their game. "You're so short that instead of tossing the ball at your waist, we'd kick it at your head," Cyrus Splinter said.

Because he was only thirty inches tall, Horace couldn't reach the Twisted Maniac and

climb into the pipes. "This game's for children thirty and one-half inches or taller," Principal Nosair said. "After you grow one half an inch, you can climb on it."

Because he was only thirty inches tall, and his eight-year-old sister Melody was on the Esophagus Eliminator, he couldn't play there either. Melody might have been two years younger than her brother, but she was one whole foot taller and almost twice as strong. In the cafeteria, she told her brother, "I'll be playing on the Esophagus Eliminator at recess, so don't even try coming near it or I'll make you eat the dust from under your bed for dinner."

To make recess even worse, Horace's best friends, Auggie and Xax Blootin, weren't at school today. The twins were both sick at home. Auggie had a cold and Xax had a severe case of Hiccupulitis. Xax had called Horace that morning. "I hiccup thirty-one times, then stop for thirty-one seconds, then start hiccuping thirty-one more times," he explained. "The only good

4

thing is that thirty-one is my favorite number."

So instead of playing at recess, Horace roamed the playground alone, looking at other kids having fun.

"My, my, what have we here?" Mr. Dienow asked. "A lone, miniature Splattly. How very, very sad." Dienow was pointy all over—pointy nose, chin, arms, legs, and even a pointy tongue. In fact, he looked like a plucked woodpecker after it had eaten rotten wood. Dienow's white hair was pulled back in a ponytail. He peered down at Horace through tiny glasses.

Horace looked up at his least-favorite teacher. Dienow taught science and was always mean to kids. Sometimes Dienow even had evil plans, like when he wanted to do experiments on the kindergartners during the Teacher Bunk-Along weekend.

"Where are the Blootin twins?" Dienow asked. "Did they get tired of having you for a friend?"

Horace raised his chin to his teacher.

"They're home sick and they'll always be my best friends," he said.

From across the playground, Noreen Limpler yelled from the Twisted Maniac, "Mr. Dienow, my foot's tangled in Bobby McGurdy's nose!"

From across the playground, Jed Breckstein yelled, "Melody Splattly won't give me a turn on the Esophagus Eliminator."

Dienow clutched the lapels of his white lab coat. "Oh, how I hate helping you kids on the playground every day. If it were up to me, we'd lock you in cages for recess," he said.

Horace gave Dienow as mean a look as he could make. "Well, fortunately, it's not up to you, and your brother's the principal," he said.

Dienow snorted. "He's only my *half* brother. We had different fathers, you toad." He crossed his arms over his chest and walked off across the playground.

Horace stood by the school, wishing recess would be over. He'd be happier tomorrow when

Auggie and Xax were back and they could investigate some of the mysteries from *The Splattly & Blootin Big Book of Worldwide Conspiracies*. They were going to start investigating why Mr. Bloddy, the school nurse, always wore his clothes inside out.

Bang. Bang. Bang.

Horace turned around and came face-to-face with Myrna Breckstein. She was swinging a large, gray lunch box against the side of the school. It had big steel bolts sticking out all over it. Myrna smiled at Horace like she'd just eaten a sack of sugar. "Now what in heaven's name are you doing standing over here, Horace Splattly?" she asked.

Earlier this year, Horace and the twins had investigated Myrna. They had thought she was really an adult pretending to be a kid. The boys had even sneaked Myrna into Mrs. Buttonslip's janitor's closet and asked her lots of questions while dripping a mop on her head. They tried to get Myrna to admit she was really forty-nine years old, but she just kept saying she was only ten. Then Mrs. Buttonslip caught them, and the three friends got punished.

Horace kicked a foot at the ground, looking at the crabgrass. "Uh, what's going on?" he asked. He leaned against the school, hoping no one had seen him talking to Myrna. He thought she acted even *weirder* than a grown-up. Maybe she was really a robot or an undersea creature that had grown legs.

Myrna held her lunch box to her stomach. "Don't you hate outdoor time?" she asked, batting her lashes at Horace. "I do. It *bores* me. I can see you're bored, too." She leaned so close to Horace that the arms of their jackets were touching. "I'm glad Auggie and Xax aren't here today," she said. "Now we can talk without them bothering us. I decided that we're going to be best friends. Don't you like that idea?" She held up her lunch box. "Do you like my new lunch box? I made it myself. Do you want to hold it?"

Horace looked at the ground. He'd rather eat

the crabgrass than talk to Myrna anymore. "Uh, not right now, thanks," he answered.

Myrna bent her knees so her face looked up at Horace. "Don't be shy, my mini-hunk. I know you only trapped me in the janitor's closet because you really like me." She gave Horace a wink. "That's why you dripped the mop on my head. It was your way of saying you wish you could mop the floors of our own home when we get married." Myrna leaned against the side of the school. "When do you want to tell everyone that you're my boyfriend?" she asked.

Horace took a step away from Myrna. She was crazy, creepy, wacky, and weird! There had to be someone he could talk to instead of her. Even *Dienow* was more fun than Myrna. "Uh, sorry, but I'm not allowed to be married or to be anyone's boyfriend," he answered. "My mom and dad said I have to wait until I'm, uh, *forty* years old." He ran across the playground and hid behind a tree. What was wrong with that girl? He couldn't believe that the twins had to be sick and leave him alone at recess.

Zap. Boom.

A bolt of lightning shot out of the sky and hit the tree over Horace's head. A huge branch crashed to the ground, the sky over the playground filled with a dark gray cloud, and raindrops the size of water balloons poured down on the kids. The strange thing was that the sky was perfectly clear except for the one cloud right above the playground. In fact, the cloud was the *exact* shape of the playground. Rain wasn't falling anywhere else.

"Everyone run inside!" Principal Nosair yelled, trying to untangle kids from the Esophagus Eliminator.

Horace dashed for the door to the school, but before he got even halfway across the playground, he had to stop. So much rain had fallen that a wide river had formed, dividing the playground in two. Most of the kids got safely into the school, but over thirty others were stranded across the river.

Principal Nosair stood inside the school and leaned out the door. Myrna Breckstein stood behind him, clutching her lunch box and smiling at the cloud above the school yard. "I'll call a construction crew to build a bridge," the principal said. He pulled the door shut and disappeared inside the school.

Horace's jeans and shirt were soaked. His spiky hair was plastered to his head.

"What'll we do?" Sara Willow cried, covering

her hair with her hands. Sara had a different hairdo every day. Today's had been in the shape of a giant sunflower when it was dry, but now the rain had made it look more like a weeping willow tree. Horace thought she was the prettiest girl he'd ever seen, even when she was as wet as a dishrag. "Where's the Cupcaked Crusader?" she asked. "He always comes to save me!"

Water dripped over Melody's face and splashed off her nose like a fountain. "That superhero better save us soon if he knows what's good for him," she said, giving her brother a look.

Horace patted his backpack. "I'll go see if I can find him," he said.

Big River

Water balloon–size raindrops crashed down on the kids as they stood on the far side of the river. The rain was cold and they huddled in a circle, wrapping their arms around one another to stay warm.

Principal Nosair leaned his head out a window. "We've called the Coast Guard!" he yelled. "They're sending a tugboat!"

The ground was so wet, the kids' feet sank into the mud up to their ankles.

Horace hid behind a bush and felt his backpack. It was wet on the outside, but he knew the inside would be dry. It held both his Cupcaked Crusader costume and a cupcake he could eat to give him powers.

He took a ball of foil from his backpack and unwrapped it. The cupcake was in the shape of a circus tent with red-and-white stripes and a flag on top. Would this give him enough powers to save the kids?

● ● ●

Horace's sister made the super-powered cupcakes. When Melody wasn't spending time bossing her brother around, she was usually in her room being a genius mad scientist, chef, and home decorator. Melody liked to use her lavender Lily Deaver Spill & Brew Science Laboratory, her lavender Lily Deaver Cook & Bake Oven, and her lavender Lily Deaver Build & Destroy Home-Construction Kit to make inventions, decorations, and foods she would test on Horace.

After school last week, Melody walked into Horace's room wearing her lavender Lily Deaver lab coat, rubber gloves, and combination hair net and portable radio. She held a sheet of lavender construction paper. "Try and take this from me," she said.

Horace was busy reading the latest edition of his favorite magazine, *Your Gym Teacher Is a Bloodsucking Toad*. "I don't want it," he answered.

Melody pulled the magazine from his hands and tossed it to the floor. "Try and grab it from me," she demanded.

"Fine," Horace said. He sat up and yanked the paper from his sister's hand. "Happy now?" he asked. A second later, the paper jumped on his face, wrapping itself around his head. A loud, piercing alarm was heard.

"Yes, I'm happy now," Melody answered with a grin.

Horace tried to peel the paper off his face. "Get it off me! Stop that noise!" No matter how hard Horace tried, he couldn't tear the paper from his head.

Melody easily plucked the paper from her

brother's face. "It would have come off on its own in ten minutes anyway. It's set on a timer," she said.

Horace breathed deeply. "Why does it do that? It's crazy!" he said. "I could have suffocated."

His sister laughed, folding the paper in half and slipping it in her lab-coat pocket. "You would not have suffocated, silly shrimp. The paper has microscopic airholes. I built a new high-tech construction paper that has a fingerprint memory sensor. That way, if anyone tries to use it but its owner, the paper will attack the criminal and the alarm will go off."

Horace picked up his magazine off the carpet. "You made a piece of construction paper that will kill people who try and take it?" he said. "Isn't that too big of a punishment for taking a piece of paper?"

Melody shrugged. "I told you, it has airholes. Besides, I think construction paper is very important for making scrapbooks, paper chains, and window decorations. I will do anything to protect *my* construction paper and believe that lots of other people feel the same way." She turned and left his room.

Horace might not have liked all of Melody's experiments, but he did think her cupcakes were pretty great. His sister mixed lots of different, weird ingredients to make special cupcakes that gave Horace superpowers. Some cupcakes made him fly, some gave him powers to shoot ice beams, and one even turned him as flat as a piece of paper. The powers would last for an hour or two, then go away. Melody also sewed Horace his superhero outfit and made him wear it whenever he ate the cupcakes. She was the person who named him the Cupcaked Crusader. "If Mom and Dad find out I'm making such dangerous cupcakes, they might take my ingredients and oven away," she told him. "Don't tell anyone you're the Cupcaked Crusader."

So far, the only people Horace had told about the cupcakes were Auggie and Xax, but he made them promise not to let Melody know that they knew. Otherwise, she might get mad and not bake him any more.

• • •

Rain pelted the playground and the children standing on it. It was raining so hard, the river had grown over ten feet wide. Neither the Coast Guard tugboat nor a bridge construction crew was anywhere in sight.

"Where oh where is the Cupcaked Crusader?" Sara moaned. "Is he abandoning us in our time of need?"

Melody looked over her shoulder to the bushes. "He better not be," she said.

Horace pulled his lavender taffeta Cupcaked Crusader costume over his school clothes. "The Cupcaked Crusader will be there in a minute!" he yelled.

He took the circus-tent cupcake in a hand and opened his mouth. Just as he was about to sink his teeth into it, a huge raindrop crashed in his eyes. "Yowwee-zowwee-zooks!" he cried. The Cupcaked Crusader stumbled, and his feet slipped out from under him. *"Yowwee-zowwee-zooks!"* Horace crashed to the ground, sending the cupcake flying out of his hand and through the air.

The superhero wiped the rain and mud out of his eyes. Where was the cupcake? He looked around where he sat in the mud. The cupcake wasn't in the bush, under his backpack, or anywhere nearby. Horace crawled to the other side of the bush.

"Look! The Cupcaked Crusader!" Petie Bloog yelled.

All the kids turned and looked at their favorite superhero.

"What are you doing crawling in the mud like a worm, Cupcaked Crusader?" Melody asked, annoyed. "Hurry up and save us."

"Uh, give me a minute," Horace replied. He looked at the river and saw it. Right by the river's edge was the red-and-white-striped circus-tent cupcake! It had landed safely on a small rock. All he had to do was sneak over, eat it, and get his powers before any of the kids saw him. Horace got down on his hands and knees and began crawling through the mud. Waves lapped at the edges of the rock, splashing the super-powered dessert. "After I have a snack, I'll save everyone," he told the kids.

Sara pointed at the cupcake. "What do you want that for?" she asked. "It's dirty in the mud. And you're not here to eat snacks, you're here to save us!"

Melody stepped forward. "Hey, don't tell a superhero what to do. If he wants to have a snack, let him," she said.

Sara shook her head. "No! He has to save us first."

Petie Bloog picked his nose then stuck his finger in his belly button. "I not heard of a superhero that eats snack before saving peoples," he said.

"This will only take a second," Horace said, strolling over to the cupcake. As he leaned over to pick it up, he slipped. Instead of grabbing the cupcake, his hand slid across the rock, shoving it into the mud. The circus-tent cupcake sank

deep into the ground, disappearing beneath its surface.

"Ha! It's gone!" Sara cried. "Now you have to save us first!"

"No! It can't be gone!" Horace cried. He dug his hands into the mud, but felt nothing. The ground had totally swallowed the cupcake.

Melody folded her arms across her chest. "You have got to be the stupidest superhero ever," she said.

"Hurry up and save us," Sheila Bamf said.

Horace faced the kids. *Thinkthinkthink*, he told himself.

But he didn't know what to do.

"Why won't you help us, Cupcaked Crusader?" Boris Nirvill asked.

Cyrus Splinter spit on the ground. "The Cupcaked Crusader's useless," he said.

Horace put his hands on his hips. "I can save you," he said. "Just watch."

The kids watched.

Melody rolled her eyes at her brother. "Okay, save us, Mr. Superhero," she said.

Horace stood on the playground. He thought long and hard, then longer and harder. His legs sank deep into the mud, up to his knees. How could he get everyone across the river and into the school without having any powers?

Lucky for the Cupcaked Crusader, before he could come up with an answer, a ladder grew out of the ground beneath him. The top rung caught the rear end of Horace's costume, lifting him high in the air.

Chapter 3

THE SUPERHERO ON THE FLYING TRAPEZE

The ladder grew out of the muddy ground, carrying the Cupcaked Crusader twenty feet in the air before it stopped growing. Horace knew that the ladder must have grown out of the circus-tent cupcake. What he didn't know was what would happen next. He hung on to the top rung, peered down at the raging river below, and waited.

"What are you doing?" Sara asked.

"I think he's trying to get away because he can't help," Cyrus Splinter said.

Horace waved to the kids. "This is all part of my plan to save you," he said in his superhero voice. A second later, a thick beam grew out of the center of the top rung and shot straight through the air across the river. Once it reached the other side, a ladder grew down to the ground and a trapeze dropped out of the center of the beam.

The rain showered harder, the ground grew muddier, and the river grew wider. If the Cupcaked Crusader was going to save the kids, he'd better start saving soon. Horace reached out and grabbed the trapeze bar. "Okay, everybody, start climbing up. I'll swing you to the other side, just like acrobats do in the circus," he said.

Melody gawked at her brother. Only she knew that he had no powers even though he was in his superhero costume. "Are you sure you know what you're doing?" she asked.

Sara grabbed the ladder and climbed up. "Of course he knows what he's doing!" she exclaimed. "He's the Cupcaked Crusader. He always saves me!"

Petie followed her. "Cupcaked Crusader is the bestest," he said.

Cyrus climbed up next. "He better know what he's doing," he said.

Horace looked at the trapeze in his hands. He'd seen acrobats do this in the circus many times, but he'd never done it himself.

Sara reached the top. "What do I do?" she asked.

Horace let go of the ladder and swung out on the trapeze. He dangled high above the river. "Grab hold of my feet," he said. "I'll take you across to the other side, then you grab the ladder on the other side, climb down, and go into the school." He kicked his legs, swinging faster and faster. Rain splashed on his hands. He clung to the bar as hard as he could. "Ready, set, go!" he called to the most beautiful girl he knew.

Sara gripped Horace's little feet in her fists and pushed off the ladder. The Cupcaked

Crusader swung her to the other side and Sara grabbed the ladder. "I made it!" she screamed. She scurried down the ladder and into the school.

Horace breathed a deep sigh of relief. Maybe he could be a superhero even without powers. Or maybe the trapeze powers were helping him. He wasn't sure, but it didn't matter—all he knew was that he had to save everyone. "See how easy it is. Who's next?" he asked.

One after another, Horace swung the kids across the river and onto the ladder at the other side. He carried the first fifteen kids across using his feet. When his legs got tired, he switched positions, hung his legs from the bar, and swung fifteen more across using his arms. After he got thirty kids across, there was only one more left to go—his sister, Melody Splattly.

She stood at the top of the ladder, facing her brother, his backpack over her shoulders. "I'm the one that makes the cupcakes, but you always save me last," she said. "Why is that?"

Horace swung back and forth between the ladders. "It's your own fault. You should have gotten in line sooner, but you didn't believe I could really help," he said. "Didn't you know the superpowers would work in the mud?"

Melody looked up at the cloud in the sky over the playground. She could see the sun shining over the rest of Blootinville. "The cupcakes are only supposed to work when eaten by people or animals," she said. "The chemicals in your saliva activate the ingredients to make them release their powers."

Horace swung up and sat on the trapeze bar. "You must be wrong," he said. "Otherwise why would the powers work in the mud?"

Melody crossed her eyes, examining a raindrop on the tip of her nose. "I don't know," she said quietly. She raised her rain-soaked face to her brother. "Now get me across!" she hollered.

Horace draped his legs over the trapeze bar. "Okay, okay, grab on," he said, extending his arms.

Melody grabbed her brother's hands, but no sooner had Horace and his sister swung over the center of the river then the two ladders on both sides began shrinking back into the ground.

"What's happening?" Melody called.

Horace held tight to his sister as the pair dropped lower and lower to the river. "The ladders are shrinking into the ground," he said. "The cupcake's powers must be wearing off."

Melody reached a leg out to grab the ladder on the side by the school. "Swing harder so we can get across," she said.

The ladders sank lower, and the tips of Melody's lavender Lily Deaver high-top sneakers touched the river. Waves crashed all around them. "Hurry!" she screamed. "Get me across and I'll share my secret stash of cupcakes with you!"

Horace swung as hard as he could. The trapeze bar tore off the center beam and Horace and Melody tumbled through the air.

Kersplot!

Melody landed in the mud by the school door.

Kersplunk!

Horace landed on top of his sister, sitting right on her head.

"Mission accomplished," he said with a laugh.

Chapter 4

THE LONG, LONG, NEVER-ENDING, LONG, LONG LIFE STORY OF DEMETRIUS DIENOW

The rain poured down, soaking Horace and his sister.

Melody stood by the side of the school, hiding her brother as he slipped out of his Cupcaked Crusader outfit.

"Hurry!" she said. "Principal Nosair is coming to the door to let us in."

"I am hurrying," Horace said. He stuffed the costume to the bottom of his backpack. When he got home that afternoon, he'd have to wash the mud out of it. He gave his sister a look. "Uh, what would have happened if I ate the cupcake? Would I have turned into a trapeze?"

Melody laughed. "Heavens, no," she answered with a smile. "You would have become a big dancing bear like in the circus."

Horace laughed. "I guess it's better I didn't eat the cupcake, then, huh?" he said. "Although maybe I could have swum across the river with kids on my back."

Principal Nosair leaned out the door. "Hurry up, kids," he said. He turned his head in every direction. "Where'd the Cupcaked Crusader go? Sara Willow said he saved all you kids."

Melody stepped through the door, taking a towel from the principal. "The Cupcaked Crusader told us he had to find a hamster that got lost in Mr. Motto's Miniature Bowling Emporium," she said.

Horace nodded. "Yep, that's what he said." He took a towel from Principal Nosair, rubbing it through his wet hair so it spiked up the way he liked it.

The principal took both kids by their shoulders and led them through the halls. "Well, you have about ten minutes before next period starts. Since it's raining, you can enjoy a special treat in the library with the rest of the school."

"Ahhhh-choooo!" Horace sneezed. "What's the special treat?"

Nosair pushed open the library door. All the kids sat quietly at the tables with frowns on their faces. Mr. Dienow sat at the front of the room reading a book that looked like it was one million pages long.

Principal Nosair whispered in the Splattly kids' ears. "My brother's reading from his biography. It's called *The Long, Long, Never-Ending, Long, Long Life Story of Demetrius Dienow*. I'm sure you'll find it very exciting." He pushed the Splattlys inside the library, then backed out of the room.

Dienow gave Horace and Melody a sour look.

"Sit," he ordered. "I just got to the part where I was one minute old."

Librarian Breckstein smiled at Horace and Melody. "I don't usually have so many kids in the library at recess," she whispered. "This is a wonderful surprise for me."

Melody tilted her head. "But isn't Mr. Breckstein the TV weatherman? He didn't say it was going to rain today."

Librarian Breckstein shook her head sadly. "Well, sometimes he makes mistakes. Weather is a tricky thing." She took the two kids and sat them at the last table with seats. "Here you go, you can sit with my own two kids. You know Jed and Myrna, don't you?"

Jed stuck his tongue out at Melody and pushed his chair away from her. "I'm going to go on the Esophagus Eliminator tomorrow and eliminate my esophagus," he said.

"I don't care what you do with your esophagus." Melody sneered. "I just want to play with *my* friends."

Librarian Breckstein shook her finger at their table. "Let Mr. Dienow read his story," she scolded.

Mr. Dienow strolled between the tables holding his enormous book. "Thank you, Ms. Breckstein. Now I'll continue." Dienow turned a page. "'When I was two minutes old, I looked at my mother and said my first words. I told my mother—'"

Cyrus raised a hand. "How could you talk if you were only two minutes old?" he asked.

"That's impossible," Sara said. "Most kids can't talk until they're two *years* old."

Dienow scowled. "I was a *much* smarter child than any of you. That's why I try to teach you, even if you can't learn. Now let me continue." He looked down to the book. "'I told mother that I would grow up to be a great scientist who would change the world and . . .'"

Myrna smiled at Horace and passed him a folded note.

Horace opened the piece of paper. It had

Myrna's name printed at the top in curly letters with tiny daisies all around the edges. It smelled as stinky as the homemade perfume his sister had once made him try. Myrna's note read:

Hi, my mini-hunk! ☺ *I wish it would* *rain* every *recess so we get to sit next to each other, don't you? Your wife-to-be, Myrny* ☺ !

Horace's face turned bright red. He quickly folded the note and hid it in a pocket.

Why did Auggie and Xax have to be sick today?

WASHOUT

All the kids in Blootinville Elementary sat in the library for the third recess in a row. Giant raindrops soaked the playground, turning it into a swampland of mud, tree limbs, and wet, moldy leaves.

Mr. Dienow pranced between the tables, reading more from his book. "'I was only forty-three minutes old, but I was still the smartest child ever,'" he read. "'My brain was the size of a large, juicy cantaloupe!'"

Myrna stared at Horace. Her wish had come

true. It was raining during all the recesses, so she could sit next to him again and again and again.

Horace thought it was a disaster.

Four days in a row, just as the kids were throwing out their lunch trash and getting ready to go outside, a rain cloud had formed over the playground. And each day, once the rain started, Principal Nosair ordered the kids into the library to sit and listen to his brother read more of his long life story. The strangest part of the rainy recess was that every day, the second the clock struck one o'clock and the bell rang for recess to end, the rain stopped, the cloud disappeared, and the sun came out again.

Dienow continued. "'At three o'clock on the first day of my life, I conducted my first science experiment. I took my bottle and squeezed it to see how far I could squirt the milk. It shot seventeen feet across the room, hitting my mommy on the back of her head.'"

Horace couldn't believe it. Dienow was as

mean when he was a baby as he was as a grown-up! Wasn't this guy ever nice? Horace propped his head on a hand and looked at the rain splashing against the library windows. Why did it rain every day only during recess and only over the school playground? He looked next to him. Myrna smiled and winked at him. Auggie and Xax were both back in school after being sick. They sat at a table across the room, covering their mouths and trying to keep from laughing at Dienow's story. Librarian Breckstein had sat them in seats on the other side of the room from Horace.

Myrna passed Horace another note. He unfolded it and read:

Hello, my mini-hunk! ☺ *I'm glad Auggie and Xax are sitting far away, so they can't bother us. Aren't you? When should we get married?*

Horace refolded the note. Just as he was

about to shove it in a pocket, a hand reached over his shoulder and snapped it from his fingers.

Dienow frowned. "Must you pass messages while I'm trying to read?" he asked.

"Sorry, Mr. Dienow," Myrna said. "I was just sharing my feelings with my boyfriend."

Kids started laughing. Melody rolled her eyes. Auggie and Xax pointed at their best friend. "She's your girlfriend?!" the boys asked at the same time.

"I think they make a cute couple," Sara said.

Dienow unfolded the note, read it to himself, and handed it to Librarian Breckstein. "It seems your daughter and Mr. Splattly plan on getting married," he said.

Myrna's mother leaned over the table and kissed both Myrna and Horace on their foreheads. "I think that's the sweetest thing I ever heard," she said.

"Awww, Mom," Myrna said, blushing.

Horace dropped his face into his hands. "May I please be excused to the bathroom?" he asked. This had to be the worst thing that had ever happened to him in school! Even worse than when he was in gym class and he bounced off the trampoline and got stuck in a basketball net.

Dienow waved Horace to the door. "Go ahead, little fella. But hurry back to your girlfriend! I don't want her to miss you too much!"

All the kids laughed again—even Xax and Auggie.

Horace walked around the table. As he passed his sister, she slipped a test tube into his pocket. "Follow my instructions," she whispered.

Horace walked out of the library and down the hall. If this rain didn't stop soon, he'd go crazy! He could not spend one more recess with Myrna Breckstein! *Not one!* She was out of control! Now all the kids thought they were boyfriend and girlfriend. Plus her mother was going to start planning the wedding!

Once Horace was safe inside the boys' room, he slipped the plastic test tube from his pocket. He took the red rubber stopper from its top and pulled out a rolled note. Melody's directions read, *Run outside and collect a fresh rain sample. I am sure something weird is going on with this rain, and I'm going to find out what it is. If I have to sit in here listening to Dienow for one more recess, I'll go mad!*

Horace smiled. He was glad his sister felt the same way he did. They might disagree about a lot of things, and she might torture him with her experiments, but at least now they were on the same side. In fact, Horace thought all the kids in school felt the same way he and Melody did. The only people who seemed to like the rainy recesses were Myrna, Mr. Dienow, and Librarian Breckstein.

Horace looked at the bathroom window. All he had to do was open it, reach out, and get a drop of water in the test tube. *Easy!* At home that afternoon, Melody would figure out what was going on so maybe she could give him a cupcake with powers to stop the rainy recesses. Sometimes it was pretty great having a mad scientist for a sister.

The window was pretty high, near the ceiling. It was the kind that had to be pushed out from the bottom so it would swing open. Horace couldn't reach it standing on the floor, so he climbed up on the sink, carefully balancing his feet along the rim. He held the test tube between his teeth and leaned forward to push open the window. Rain beat down against the glass, making it hard for him to swing it wide. He pressed his palms flat against the window and pushed with all his might.

Eeeeeeeeekkkkkkkkkkkkkk!

The good news was, the window flipped wide open. The bad news was that Horace had pushed so hard, he couldn't stop himself from flying forward and out the window.

Splop!

Horace dropped to the ground outside the library windows. But that didn't matter. All that mattered was that he had to get a fresh rain sample. He knelt on the ground and unplugged the test tube, letting rain fall in the top. He plugged the top of the test tube closed with the stopper and slipped it in his pocket. When he stood to go back inside, he saw that he was covered from head to toe with mud. Worse yet, everyone in the library was standing at the windows laughing at him.

Well, everyone was laughing, except for one librarian, one teacher, and one kid.

Librarian Breckstein ran around the room trying to quiet the kids and get them back to their seats.

Myrna clasped her hands to her head. "Are you okay, my mini-hunk?" she yelled through the window.

Dienow leaned over her shoulder and swung a window open.

"To the Detention Cage, Mr. Splattly!" he yelled at Horace. "Now!"

THE CAGED SPLATTLY ALWAYS SINGS

"I hate to punish students, but for your own safety, you must behave," Principal Nosair said, locking Horace in the Detention Cage. The principal lectured all the kids in the hallway. "Horace Splattly put himself in danger by climbing out a window in the middle of a terrible rainstorm. He's so little, he could have easily fallen in a puddle and drowned." The principal gave Horace a stern look. "Now sing the Detention Cage song, then everyone will go to their afternoon classes."

Horace stood inside the Detention Cage outside Principal Nosair's office. He clung to the cage's bars. Mud hardened all over him, making his clothes stiff and his face crinkly like dry clay. The cage was made of thick stalks of celernip that had been bound with rope. Kids were only put in the Detention Cage if they had broken a rule that worried the teachers. Whoever was put in the cage had to sing the special Detention Cage song.

All the kids and teachers waited for Horace to begin. Cyrus Splinter laughed. "He looks like a muddy gerbil," he teased.

Myrna clapped her hands to her cheeks. "Oh, my honey bun, why'd you do it?" she cried. "Weren't we having fun sitting together in the library?"

Auggie and Xax got close enough to the cage to speak to their friend.

"Why were you climbing out the window?" Auggie asked.

"Was the bathroom smelly, so you were trying to let in fresh air?" Xax asked.

Principal Nosair led the twins farther away from the cage. "That's enough chitchat. Horace is being punished," he said. "Let him sing the song."

Horace tried to open his mouth. Bits of mud rolled off his lip and onto his tongue. "Can I just speak the song instead of singing it?" he asked.

The principal shook his head. "You know the rule."

Ms. Tiborfarlin wheeled her piano out of the music room and into the hallway. "Are you ready?" she asked.

"Uh, okay," Horace said.

The music teacher pounded her hands on the piano keys and Horace began singing.

"I'm a Little Detention Boy,
In a Big Detention Cage.
I didn't listen to the rules,
So now I'm punished in my school.
I'm a Little Detention Boy,
Poop-poop-dee-doo!"

Horace kicked up his heels and bowed, looking out at the crowd. No one applauded. No one even smiled.

"He's not a very good singer," Sara whispered to Missy Boil.

Principal Nosair clapped his hands. "Okay, show's over. Off to your classes."

The kids and teachers filed into their classrooms. Xax and Auggie hung back by the cage.

"So why'd you do it?" Xax asked.

"What's the scoop?" Auggie asked. "Now that everyone's gone, you can tell us."

Melody pushed her way between the twins. "Did you get the sample?" she asked.

Horace nodded.

"What sample?" Xax asked.

"None of your business," Melody snapped. She winked at her brother and ran into her classroom.

"A sample of what?" Auggie asked.

Horace knelt to get closer to the boys so no one else would hear. A clump of dried mud dropped off his cheek to the cage's floor.

Xax reached in and picked it up. "This looks like Eleanor Roosevelt," he said. "I'm going to have Mr. Paul fire it in the kiln so I can paint it."

Auggie shoved his brother aside. "What's Melody up to?" he asked.

"I got a fresh water sample from the rain," Horace said. "Come to my house this afternoon and we can start the Official Investigation of the Rainy Recesses."

THE INVESTIGATION BEGINS

The Splattly house was silent.

Horace and Auggie lay sprawled across the bedroom floor with *The Splattly & Blootin Big Book of Worldwide Conspiracies* open between them. Auggie was carefully outlining letters at the top of the page with the name of the investigation. Horace was labeling photos the boys had taken of the muddy playground. Xax typed at Horace's computer keyboard, searching the Internet for information about rainy recesses.

Melody was in her room testing the rain sample Horace had gotten from the playground puddle. Horace and Melody's dad was working in his office around the side of the Splattly home. Dr. Hinkle Splattly was a psychiatrist. He helped people who had problems with friends, families, and jobs and needed to talk to someone. Dr. Splattly checked in on his kids in between his sessions with patients to make sure they were behaving. Horace and Melody's mom was at work. Mari Splattly was the publisher of the town newspaper, *The Blootinville Banner*. She wouldn't get home until seven o'clock.

"Has anything like this happened at any other schools?" Horace asked Xax.

Xax stared at a photo on the computer of a herd of llamas running through the halls of a school in Brazil. He clicked to another Web page and saw a photo of a school in Taiwan that had been covered with pancake batter. Xax clicked off the computer. "There's nothing about rainy school playgrounds, but there sure are a lot of other interesting things happening," he said.

Horace taped the photos onto the page of the notebook. "It must be an inside job," he said.

Auggie colored in the letters he had outlined with blue marker. "But how could anyone make it rain whenever he wanted to?" he asked.

"And how could someone make it rain only over the playground?" Xax asked.

Horace got into his thinking pose. He stuck the forefinger of his right hand in his ear and the forefinger of his left hand on his chin.

Xax did a somersault on the floor and bumped into the wall. "What about Cyrus Splinter?" he asked. "He's always mean and likes to ruin everyone's fun."

"He *is* mean," Auggie said. "But he's not smart enough to make it rain."

Xax did a reverse somersault and crashed into Horace's coatrack. An umbrella fell off and popped open on his head.

"Sit still, lumber brain," Auggie told his twin. "It's hard to think when you're moving around."

Xax pouted. "But I do my best thinking when I do gymnastics," he said.

"Then do it quietly," Auggie told him.

Horace shut his eyes and stayed in his think-

ing pose. *Thinkthinkthink*, he told himself. Who was smart enough to make it rain and would also *want* to make it rain? *WhoWhoWho?*

Only one name came to Horace's mind—the most evil man in all of Blootinville Elementary School.

"Mr. Dienow!" Horace exclaimed. "It has to be him!"

Xax did a cartwheel across the floor, landing atop Horace's bed. "He has to be the one!" Horace said. "He wants it to rain so we have to listen to him read his book every day in the library!"

"I think you're right," Auggie agreed. He picked up a red marker, wrote *Suspects* on the page and drew a box around it. Underneath it, he wrote *Demetrius Dienow, Science Teacher at Blootinville Elementary School*.

Horace stared at the name in the book. "We have to call the police on him," he said. "This can't go on."

"But we don't have any proof," Auggie said.

Xax looked out the window. "And how can we be sure that the rain over the playground isn't just some weird weather thing?" he asked. "I've heard of places in South America where it rains every day, all the time. Maybe the playground is like that."

The three boys looked at one another. They had a mystery and they had a suspect, but they didn't have a way to prove Dienow was doing it.

Horace looked at the notebook, shook his head, and closed it. "Maybe you're right, Xax. Maybe this is just a weird weather thing," he said.

Just then, Horace's bedroom door flew open and Melody stood in the entrance wearing her lavender Lily Deaver lab coat and carrying two Lily Deaver test tubes in her hands. "Don't close the book on this conspiracy too fast, boys. I think I have our first bit of evidence."

Horace sat up. "What did you discover?" he asked.

Melody held up one test tube filled with ice.

"This test tube contained normal rainwater. When I added a special freeze chemical to it, it turned to ice just like normal water would." She tucked that test tube in the pocket of her lab coat and held the other test tube before the boys' faces. It was filled with a steamy, bubbly blue liquid. "When I added the freeze chemical to the rainwater from the playground, the water didn't freeze. It changed color and began boiling."

Xax touched the tip of his finger to the test tube. "Yow! That's hot! Real water would freeze at thirty-two degrees Fahrenheit. I know that because it's one degree warmer than my favorite degree."

Melody nodded. "Exactly! This does the opposite of what real water would do. Someone must have invented some kind of machine that can develop clouds that shower fake rain on the playground. There aren't too many people as smart as me who could make such an invention. Whoever made those rain clouds must be a genius."

"An *evil* genius," Horace said.

Auggie looked to him. "So what do we do?" he asked. "Should we still investigate Mr. Dienow?"

Melody wrinkled her mouth. "Do you think he's smart enough to make an invention like this? I'm not sure."

Horace grabbed his jacket off the closet doorknob. "I think we'd better go spy on him and find out," he said. "When Dad checks in, tell him I'm out riding bikes with Xax and Auggie. I'm sure Dienow's the one who's making the rainy recesses. He's really, really evil."

Melody waved the test tube in Horace's face. "But I don't think he's an evil *genius*. I just think he's a mean teacher. There's a big difference."

Auggie and Xax put on their jackets and picked up their backpacks. "Well, let's go find out," he said. "If we're wrong, we'll just have to find another suspect."

Xax looked from Auggie to Horace to Melody. "Uh, but what happens if he *is* the one doing it?" he asked. "What'll we do to stop him? What if he catches us and tries to send us into the sky in one of his fake clouds?"

Horace handed Xax his jacket and backpack. "We're just going to spy on him, Xax. We're not going to talk to him," he said.

"Promise?" Xax asked.

"Uh, sure," Horace said, not sure that he could really keep the promise.

Melody pulled Horace aside and turned to the twins. "Now, you two, head downstairs and wait for my brother. I have something to tell him."

Auggie folded his arms across his chest. "If we're part of this investigation, we need to know everything that Horace knows," he said.

Xax folded his arms across his chest just like his brother. "Yeah," he said. "Everything."

Melody tilted her head to the twins. "Do you really want to hear my instructions on how I want Horace to wash my underwear?" she asked.

Auggie and Xax gritted their teeth. "Uh, I don't think we need to know about that," Auggie said.

"No way," Xax said.

The twins dashed out the door of Horace's bedroom.

Horace sighed. "Geez, Melody, did you have to embarrass me like that?"

Melody shrugged. "I had to get rid of them somehow. I wanted to tell you that while you're out spying on Mr. Dienow, I'll be busy making you a superpowered cupcake so you can stop the cloud from raining at recess tomorrow."

Horace didn't tell his sister that Auggie and Xax already knew about the cupcakes. That was the secret he and the twins shared. "Sounds great," he said. "It's a lot better than giving me instructions on how to wash your underwear."

Melody gave her brother's shoulder a squeeze. "I'll give you directions on how to do *that* when you get home," she said.

Chapter 8

BEWARE OF THE ANT

Whoooooooooooooooooooooooooooooosh!

Mr. Dienow's house stood at the end of a runway by the Blootinville International Airport and Town Dump. It was a gray cement block with a glass dome on top. It sat in the middle of a patch of dry dirt surrounded by dead, brown bushes. Planes and helicopters were constantly roaring overhead as they took off and landed on the runways. The only way inside the house was through a gray steel door with fifteen locks. Two cameras were stuck on the front corners of the house, watching for anyone who might go near it.

Horace, Xax, and Auggie hid their bikes in a pile of cans across the street at the dump. They lay flat on their stomachs, wriggling across the road like worms until they were safely hidden behind a row of dead bushes.

"Ouch!" Xax pulled a prickly twig from his hair. "How are we ever going to get in there?"

Auggie picked up a rock and tossed it into the middle of Dienow's yard. The camera spun around and aimed right at it. A voice boomed from a speaker above the front door. "*Stay away!*

The owner of this house is not friendly! Stay away!" a recording announced.

"There's no way to peek in," Xax said. He began backing across the street to his bike.

Auggie grabbed his hand and pulled him forward. "We can't give up so easy," he said.

"There has to be another way in. Maybe there's a back door or a basement window or something," Horace said. He crept around the edge of the bushes, followed by Auggie and Xax. Once they reached the back of the house,

Horace pushed his head between the bushes. "Well, I found our way in," he told the twins.

Auggie and Xax peered through the bushes.

"I don't see a door," Xax said.

"I don't see a window," Auggie said.

Horace pointed to a pipe that ran up the back of the house to the roof. "The drainpipe will take us up to the roof. Then we'll be able to see inside through the glass dome. Since there aren't any cameras back here, Dienow won't know we're trying to spy on him. It's perfect!"

Auggie and Xax looked at each other then at Horace.

"We can't climb up that pipe," Xax said. "I'm afraid of pipes."

"Since when?" Horace asked.

"Since they were attached to Mr. Dienow's house," Xax said.

Auggie sat in the dirt. "Listen, Horace. We want to find out if Dienow's the one doing it, too, but we thought we'd just be able to look in his front window. Xax and I didn't think we'd have to climb up on his roof. That's almost like we're burglars."

Horace gasped. "But what he's doing is far worse than climbing on his roof!" he said. "He's making it rain on our playground so we have to listen to him read his life story!"

"We don't even have proof he did it," Auggie said. "Xax and I are the mayor's sons. It would be a scandal if we were caught on Dienow's roof."

"Exactly," Xax agreed. "Everyone in town could say our dad can't be mayor anymore. Remember how angry he got when we flopped around on the floor of Mr. Howlly's doughnut shop pretending we were fish because we thought he was a walrus?"

"Our dad still hasn't forgiven us for that," Auggie said. "Sorry, Horace, but we can't climb up on the roof of Dienow's house."

Horace got into his thinking pose. He thought long and hard, then longer and harder. "Okay," he told the twins. "I understand. You can't, but I can. Here's how you can help me. Both of you go around and knock on Dienow's front door and keep him busy talking about school. That's when I'll climb up the pipe and peek down to see if he's doing any weather experiments. Deal?"

Xax looked to his brother. "I don't think knocking on a door will get us into trouble," he said.

Auggie looked at his brother. "I don't think talking to Dienow about school will get us into trouble," he said.

"Great!" Horace said. "So let's put this plan into action."

The twins crawled around the edge of the yard, hiding behind the bushes. Horace watched them go, then made his move. He dashed through the bushes, across Dienow's yard, and pressed himself flat against the house by the drainpipe.

"Stay away! The owner of this house is not friendly! Stay away!"

Horace heard the recording and knew his friends must be by Dienow's front door. He reached for the pipe, grabbed hold, and pulled himself up the side of the concrete house.

"What's going on?! Who's out there?!" Mr. Dienow's voice boomed from inside the house.

"Hi, Mr. Dienow. It's just us Blootins. We thought we'd come for a visit," Auggie said.

"We like your book so much, we wanted to see where you lived in real life," Xax said.

Horace reached the top of the pipe, climbed atop the house, and slid his body to the center of the dome.

Whooooooooooooooooooooooooooosh. A plane roared. It flew so low, Horace was sure it clipped a lock of hair off his head. He stretched out his arms and legs and held tight to the glass. He looked down at the inside of Dienow's home.

He could see his science teacher standing by the front door with Auggie and Xax.

Dienow leaned over the twins. "Leave me alone! This isn't school. If it rains next recess, you'll hear more of my story!" He reached out to slam the door.

Auggie pushed it back with a hand. "Do you think it will rain tomorrow?" he asked.

Xax put his hand up to help keep the door open. "Do you know how to make it rain so we'll get to stay in and hear more of your story?" he asked.

Dienow slapped the boys' hands off his door and got ready to close it. "Watch Weatherman Breckstein on TV! He can tell you more about rain! I'm in the middle of an important experiment! I'm trying to come up with a formula that turns little, annoying boys into gumdrops!" He reached to slam the door shut.

"Wait!" Auggie said. "There's one more thing!"

Dienow stared down the length of his pointy nose at the twins. "What?!"

Auggie kicked his shoe at the "Unwelcome" mat in front of Dienow's door. "Uh, Mr. Dienow, sir, we were just wondering if you'd like a statue of yourself in the town center. Right, Xax?"

Xax nodded quickly. "That's right. We think you're so interesting, we told our dad that you deserve one."

Dienow pulled on his pointy chin. "Hmm . . . a statue of me in the town square? Very interesting," he said, leaning against the doorframe. "My brother doesn't have a statue in the town square."

While the twins and Dienow talked about whether the statue should be made of gold, marble, or diamonds, Horace peered into the home below.

The house was one giant room. The kitchen was in one corner. A bed was in another corner, and the living and bathroom areas were in other corners. Right in the center of the room was a laboratory. Giant tubes twisted in every direction with different-colored liquids flowing through them. Some of the tubes spit liquid up at the ceiling, splattering the glass. Weird vines climbed the walls, oozing sap that dripped down to the floor. A lot of weird stuff was going on, but nothing that looked like it could make rain clouds.

A strange ant crawled across the inside of the glass dome. It had a yellow head, green body, and orange tail. "Hey, little fella," Horace told the tiny insect. "I bet you wish you were out here with me."

The insect crawled right up to Horace's face. The ant had a mean look in its eye and seemed to understand every word Horace had said. The ant even opened its mouth like it was going to talk.

"Go ahead. Say something," Horace joked. "Does Dienow have a weather machine?"

"AAAAAAYYYYYYIIIIIIIEEEEEEEEEEEE!" the ant shrieked. The ant's scream was as loud as one thousand sirens.

Horace looked down and saw Dienow turn and look up at the glass dome.

"You awful children!" Dienow gritted his teeth, scowled at the twins, and slammed the door in their faces.

"AAAAAYYYYYIIIIIIIEEEEEEEEEEEE!" the ant shrieked again.

Dienow walked to the center of the room. "That's enough, Theodore!" he told the ant. "Down now!" The tiny insect leaped down from the glass and landed on the teacher's shoulder.

Horace slid down the glass, trying to get away as fast as possible.

But he wasn't fast enough.

Dienow pulled a large lever by his desk and the glass dome began spinning in a circle. "Who's that up there?" he asked, gazing at the glass roof. "Do you think you can spy on me and get away with it?"

The dome spun faster, like a carnival ride. The world became a blur before Horace's eyes. He clung to the glass as tight as he could, but no matter how hard he tried, he couldn't hold on. His hands slid from the glass and he felt himself fly off the dome.

"Ha-ha-ha-ha-ha!" Dienow chuckled.

Horace flew through the air, twisting and turning in every direction. He fell faster and faster, knowing that he'd soon hit the ground and be broken into a million billion pieces.

Plooooooooof!

Horace crashed on something soft. In fact, it was the softest thing he'd ever felt in his life! He looked down. He'd landed on a giant pile of old feather pillows in the garbage dump.

"Horace, where are you?" Xax and Auggie called.

"I'm up here," Horace answered.

A minute later, Xax and Auggie stood at the bottom of the pillow hill. They must have seen Horace fly off Dienow's roof and into the dump. "So did you find out anything?" Xax asked.

Horace sat up and shook the dizzies from his head. "Uh, well, I didn't find out for sure if Dienow had a weather machine or not, but I did learn one thing," he said.

"What's that?" Auggie asked.

Horace slid down the pile of pillows. "I don't ever want to climb on the roof of Dienow's house again," he said.

Chapter 9

THE CUPCAKED CRUSADER MEETS HIS MATCH

"**K**ids, stop staring at the TV. It's time to go to school," Dr. Splattly called into the living room.

Horace and Melody stood in front of the TV, dressed for school, with their backpacks slung over their shoulders. Neither of them moved an inch as they watched a commercial for Pleary: The Family Game of Earwax.

"We're waiting to watch the weather report," Melody said.

"We have to see if it's going to rain at recess," Horace said.

Mrs. Splattly stepped into the room carrying her briefcase. "Out you go. Stop dillydallying," she said.

Horace and Melody stood rooted to their spots. Finally, Weatherman Breckstein appeared on the TV. He looked very serious and pointed at a map of Blootinville. "Okay, here's the school-day weather report. There will be no rain at Blootinville Elementary today. I know I was wrong the last three days, but today there really won't be a rainy recess." He took out a smiley sun and slapped it right on the map where the school playground was. "There isn't a cloud within one hundred miles of the school today. There's no way it can rain."

Mrs. Splattly switched off the TV. "See? No rain. Now head off to school," she said.

Melody and Horace walked out the front door and looked up at the sky.

"Do you think Weatherman Breckstein's right?" Horace asked. "Do you think the rainy recesses were just some weird weather thing that happened and Dienow had nothing to do with them?"

Melody scoffed at her brother. "My experiments indicate that the rain is man-made. Someone has to be making those clouds and you can't really be sure it's not Dienow, can you?" she said. "You really didn't find anything out when you went to his house. Let this be a lesson to you—without my superpowered cupcakes . . . you're *nothing*. Obviously you need a genius like me to turn you into a superhero or you can't get anything done."

Horace stopped on the sidewalk. "I am sure it's not Dienow," he said. "He said he was busy working on an experiment to turn kids into candy."

Melody glared at her older brother, putting her hands on her hips. "But you don't know that for sure," she said. "He might have lied to Xax and Auggie. And you couldn't tell what kind of experiment he was doing from what you saw." She reached into her backpack and took out a cupcake in a small, plastic bag. "Here. Eat this for dessert at lunch, then rush into the bathroom and put on your Cupcaked Crusader costume. This will give you the powers you need to get up in the cloud and learn what's going on. Maybe then you'll really be able to find out whether Dienow's the one doing this or not." Melody ran up the sidewalk, leaving her brother far behind.

Horace stuffed the cupcake in his backpack, watching his sister grow smaller and smaller the farther she ran. "I know it wasn't Dienow," he said aloud, but deep inside, he really wasn't sure.

• • •

"Hey, give me that! You can have my dessert— it's a piece of toast with mustard and sugar on top." Cyrus Splinter leaned over Horace's lunch table and reached for the cupcake Melody had made.

Horace snatched the superpowered cupcake up and held it to his chest. "You can't! My sister made it special for me," he said.

Cyrus, Michael Ma, and Saul Shlock stood over the lunch table where Horace sat with the twins. "Oh, isn't that just cute?" Cyrus sneered. "Your sister made you a fancy dessert!" He stuck his big hand in Horace's face. "And I want it!"

Horace hunched forward, curling his body around the cupcake. "Get away from me!" he told him.

"Back off!" Auggie said.

Hearing the arguing, Lunch Lady McCaffrey bustled over to the table. She was almost eighty years old, had the body of a football player, and

the face of a sweet, old lady. "Okay, boys, move along. Eat lunch at your own table," she told the bullies, shooing them away.

Cyrus, Michael, and Saul slinked away and took their seats at the far side of the room.

Horace took the superpowered cupcake out of the plastic bag and sat it on the table. "What do you think of it?" he asked.

The three boys examined the cupcake, leaning so close to it that their noses were almost touching the icing. The cupcake looked and smelled like a plain vanilla cupcake with vanilla frosting and blue sprinkles on top. There was nothing very strange or different about it at all.

"Are you sure it has powers?" Auggie asked.

Horace inspected the blue sprinkles. Were they moving or was it just his imagination? "Melody said it did and I don't think she'd fake me out," he said. "She wants the rainy recesses to end as much as we do." He picked up the cupcake. "I guess there's only one way to find out what will happen." He opened his mouth and popped the vanilla cupcake in.

"Well?" Auggie asked.

"Anything strange happening?" Xax asked.

Horace chewed. The second the cupcake touched his tongue, it became slimy and oily. The cupcake tasted like he was licking the floor of a garage and sucking on a car exhaust pipe at the same time.

He felt like he was being poisoned. Sharp stabbing pains came from his stomach, bounced around his insides, then stabbed at his heart. Horace clutched his chest.

"Horace? Are you all right?" Xax asked.

Outside, the sunny day quickly turned dark and cloudy.

Kra-boom!

A lightning bolt exploded from the cloud, thunder clapped, and rain drenched the playground.

Another rainy recess had begun.

"Not again!" a bunch of kids moaned.

Horace felt like he was going to drop dead, but he had to get his Cupcaked Crusader costume on before any superpowers started to activate. He picked up his backpack off the floor. "I'll talk to you guys later," he said. "I—I think I—" He lurched out of the cafeteria and into the hallway.

The boys' bathroom was across the hall, but the pain in his body was so terrible, Horace couldn't take another step. His knees buckled and he fell to the floor, rolling his body behind a trash can so no one would see him.

He was dying. He was sure of it. He was going to die right here behind a trash can in the hallway of Blootinville Elementary! His sister had made a mistake and poisoned him with one of her cupcakes.

Horace unzipped his backpack and put on the Cupcaked Crusader costume, hoping the pain would stop and the powers would come.

But that didn't happen. All he felt was that his body was becoming hollow, as if everything inside him was crumbling apart. Horace took a pen and piece of paper from his backpack. The time had come to write a farewell note to his parents.

Kra-boom!

Lightning flashed through the windows, thunder roared, waves of rain poured down over the playground.

Principal Nosair announced over the school's loudspeaker, *"Okay, kids, because of the rain, you'll spend recess in the library hearing more of my brother's life story."*

Horace put his pen to the paper and wrote:

Dear Mom and Dad,

It was nice knowing you. Thanks for being a good mom and dad. Just to let you know, Melody poisoned me, so if you want to blame anyone for me dying, you can blame her. Maybe you should take away her Lily Deaver oven and science laboratory.

Love and good-bye,

Your son, Horace

P.S. I was also the

Before he could finish his letter, his arms suddenly turned into hollow tubes and sucked in air, making his body inflate like a balloon. The pen he held disappeared up his arm and Horace could feel it floating inside his body. He waved an arm in the air and sucked a poster off the wall announcing the kindergartners' school play, *Mary Had a Little Lamb but Then She Ate It*. The poster crumpled into a ball and whooshed up Horace's arm into his body.

He'd become a human vacuum cleaner!

Horace closed his armholes so he wouldn't suck anything more inside him. He knew exactly what he had to do. He would just point his arms at the cloud and suck it right inside him. That would stop the rainy recess!

He pushed open a door and ran onto the soggy playground. Rain poured down, soaking his costume.

"The Cupcaked Crusader's here!" Petie Bloog shouted.

"He can stop the rainy recesses!" Sara Willow yelled.

All the kids in Blootinville Elementary pressed their noses to the cafeteria windows

along with Principal Nosair, Librarian Breckstein, Mr. Dienow, and the other teachers.

Horace bowed. "I'll stop this rain so everyone
can come out and play!" he told the school. He
raised his arms in the air and was about to suck
the rain cloud out of the sky when he heard a
whirring sound and saw someone fly off the roof
of the school and swoop down at him. It was a
girl in a black dress and high black boots. A red
heart was on the middle of her costume in the
front, and her face was covered with a black
mask that had hearts for eyeholes. She wore a
jetpack on her back and flew down to where
Horace stood.

"Not so fast, Cupcaked Crusader," the girl said.

Horace stared at the girl. Who was she?
Where had she come from?

"Hello, Cupcaked Crusader, cat got your
tongue?" the girl asked. She leaned in so close to
Horace, he could smell tuna salad on her breath.
"I don't think you should be ending our rainy
recesses. Not if you know what's good for you."

Horace took a step back and prepared to open his armholes. "Why should I listen to you?" he asked in his loudest Cupcaked Crusader voice. "Who do you think you are to stop me?"

The girl flew circles around Horace. "I'm the Heartbreaker. I'm the genius who made the rainy recesses and I'm not going to stop making them," the girl said. "Now here's the choice *you* have to make: You can either join me and we can control Blootinville Elementary together, or you can try and fight me." She flew down to Horace and gave his cheek a kiss. "I think you're a real cute superhero," she whispered in his ear. "But if you try and fight me, I'll destroy you." The Heartbreaker flew high in the air and out of sight.

"Stop her!" kids yelled from the cafeteria.

"Don't let her get away!"

"Make her stop doing this!"

Horace turned his head in every direction. Where had the Heartbreaker come from? Where had she flown off to?

Melody knocked on the cafeteria window. "Hey, Cupcaked Crusader, less smooching and more action!" she called.

Horace looked at his sister, then to his hands, remembering that he was a superhero and had to stop the rainy recess no matter what the Heartbreaker said.

He raised his arms over his head and opened his vacuum hand holes.

Swoooooooooooooooooooooooooooooooosh!

Within seconds, the cloud above the playground was sucked up through the Cupcaked Crusader's arms along with broken tree branches, leaves, and a bird's nest with a family of sparrows in it. The sky above the school was clear during recess for the first time in days. The bright sun immediately began drying the muddy ground.

The kids in the cafeteria cheered.

The only problem was that now that Horace had sucked up so much stuff, his body had inflated to become nearly twenty feet high with his normal-size arms and legs and head attached. He could feel the birds flying around inside him, trying to find a way out.

A light wind blew, rolling the Cupcaked Crusader across the playground and tangling him in the Esophagus Eliminator.

Horace kept his armholes closed so he wouldn't suck in anything more. If he did, he was sure he would explode like an overfilled balloon. How was he supposed to get rid of the cloud inside him so he could return to his normal size?

All the kids ran out across the playground, surrounding him. They lifted Horace over their heads and tossed him back and forth. "Hip-hip, hooray for the Cupcaked Crusader! Hip-hip, hooray!" they cheered.

"Uh, be careful with your fingernails," Horace told the kids. "Don't pop me!"

"Good work, Cupcaked Crusader," Principal Nosair said.

Mr. Dienow gave the superhero a poke with a finger. "Finally, I don't have to waste my time reading to the kids in the library," he said.

Librarian Breckstein looked up at the clear sky. "I liked having the kids in the library, but it's better that they get to play outside," she said.

The kids tossed Horace high in the sky and a wind picked him up, lifting him in the air and over the school.

"Awww, now we can't play with him anymore," Sara Willow said.

Principal Nosair wagged a finger at the girl.

"The Cupcaked Crusader is not a toy," he reminded her. "He's a superhero and he has important things to do."

The wind carried Horace to the school's roof, where he landed on a pile of rags the janitor had put out to dry.

Now, how was he going to return to normal? That's when he noticed it—a small switch on one of his armholes marked REVERSE.

Of course! He had a reverse switch! He should have known Melody would have thought of that.

Horace rolled his body to an exhaust pipe coming out of the cafeteria roof and hooked the switch against its opening, giving it a tug.

Vrrrrrooooooooooooooooooooooooooooooooo ooooooom!

Everything that had been inside the Cupcaked Crusader blew out his armholes and across the roof. Horace's body shrank back to its normal size and his vacuum arms instantly turned back to boy arms and hands. The family of birds flew around his head, tweeting happily.

Horace walked over to the door that led down into the school. He'd just sneak in while everyone was at recess, put his Cupcaked Crusader costume away, and join everyone outside.

Just as Horace opened the door, he heard a whirring sound and looked up to see the Heartbreaker flying above his head. "You may have won this round, Cupcaked Crusader, but I know you'll start liking me soon. Why would you want to have powers alone when together we could have much more fun?" she asked. "Now let's find out who you really are." She reached out a hand to pull off Horace's mask.

Horace gasped and shoved the Heartbreaker's hand away.

The Heartbreaker laughed a high, shrill laugh. "Okay, so you don't want to reveal yourself in the light of day? Then meet me atop the weather tower above Crawlyworm Falls at midnight tonight and we can make a plan to take over the school." She leaned in to give Horace a kiss on the cheek, but Horace was too fast for her. He turned and dashed inside the school, slamming the door behind him. "I'll never join you!" he yelled through the door. "Never!"

But deep inside, Horace wasn't so sure. Would having powers be more fun if he did it with someone else? Maybe the Heartbreaker could give him powers so he wouldn't have to ask his little sister for the cupcakes . . . He remembered how that very morning Melody had said he was nothing without her . . .

Would he be more powerful if he teamed up with the Heartbreaker?

Horace wondered.

Chapter 10

WHO'S THAT GIRL?

After school, the three boys lay in the shade of a tree in the town square. Auggie busily wrote all about the Heartbreaker in *The Splattly & Blootin Big Book of Worldwide Conspiracies*. "What should we do next?" he asked. "How can we find out who she is?"

Xax opened the Blootinville Elementary School yearbook and flipped through the pages. "There are exactly two hundred thirty-eight girls in the school, not including the grown-ups. If you count them, too, then there are exactly two hundred and seventy-three girls in the school," he reported.

Auggie took the yearbook and held a page up to Horace. "Do you recognize anyone?" he asked.

Horace stared at a row of photos of kids from the first grade. "Do you think a first grader could be the genius who's making this happen?" he asked.

Xax nodded. "Your sister's in second grade and look what she can do," he said.

Auggie turned a page to a class of kindergartners. "Our dad told us about one five-year-old who was so smart that he ran a whole country," he said.

Horace studied the faces of the girl kindergartners and slapped a hand to the side of his head. "I can't believe it!" he said. He took the book and slammed it shut.

"What?" Auggie asked. "Why aren't you looking at the pictures?"

Horace frowned. "The only part of her I got to see was her eyes, but I can't even remember what color they are," he said. "How could I be so stupid?"

Melody stood above the boys. "Why are you wasting your time trying to figure out who the Heartbreaker is? Does it matter?" she asked.

Xax sat up. "Of course it matters. We have to catch her," he said.

Melody tossed up her hands. "Don't be idiotic! It doesn't matter *who* she is. All that matters is that she's stopped," she said. "Now come along, Horace, I need you to help me take care of some *chores* at home. I'm doing some new experiments and I want you to be my *assistant*."

Horace stood and faced his sister. "Maybe I don't want to help you with your experiments," he said.

Melody poked a finger at her brother's chest. "If you want a delicious after-school *treat* or maybe some *cake* after dinner, you'd better come home with me *now*," she warned.

Horace knew she was talking about the cupcakes, but he wasn't in the mood to be bossed around by his little sister. At least not today. "I'm not going anywhere with you," he said. *"We're* going to figure out who's doing this. That's our plan and *that's* what I'm going to do."

"Yeah, he's staying with us," Xax said.

Melody turned up her nose at the twins and faced her brother. "You're just wasting your time with the Blootins. Come home with me now," she ordered.

Horace stood his ground. "NO!" he yelled. "You go home alone!" He turned and sat back under the tree, burying his face behind the yearbook. He could hear Melody make a loud

harrumph and stomp away. After a moment, he raised his head, peeking from behind the book's pages. "Uh, is she gone?" he whispered to the twins.

"Gone for good," Auggie answered.

"*Phew*," Xax said, wiping his hand across his brow. "She's the scariest, bossiest girl I know."

Horace nodded. "But not the *meanest*. The Heartbreaker is the real villain, and we have to find out who she is."

"But if you don't know what she looks like, how can we find out who she is?" Xax asked.

Horace thought long and hard, then longer and harder. Then he told his friends the one thing he hadn't mentioned. "The Heartbreaker wants me to meet her at the top of the weather tower at Crawlyworm Falls to take off our masks together. She wants me to team up with her so we can be more powerful and take over the school together."

"You can't team up with her!" Auggie said.

"She's evil!" Xax exclaimed. "And if she finds

out who you are, she could come after you, your family, and all your friends like Auggie and me. Your parents might even make Melody stop making the cupcakes because they'll think it's too dangerous for you to be a superhero."

Horace nodded. "That's true. But maybe we can make a plan and trick her into taking off her mask without me taking off mine," he said.

Xax leaped to his feet. "Eureka!" he cheered, proudly raising his arms in the air. "I've got our solution! We can make a fake Cupcaked Crusader and put him on top of the weather tower! Then we can attach a microphone to him, so you could talk to the Heartbreaker while the three of us hide somewhere. Then you could get her to take off her mask, and when she takes off yours, she'll just see a dummy."

Auggie smiled and clapped a hand on his brother's back. "You know, I think that's the best idea you've ever had," he said. "That brain in your head works in pretty mysterious ways."

"That *is* a good plan," Horace agreed.

Xax stared at the ground, looking very serious. "Forty-two, forty-three, forty-four," he counted.

"Is something wrong?" Horace asked.

Auggie shook his head. "I think our mastermind is busy counting every blade of grass in the town square," he explained.

Chapter 11

THE VAULT

Horace stood over his sister as she worked at her lavender Lily Deaver Spill & Brew Science Laboratory. "Why won't you give me any cupcakes? Don't you want to stop the Heartbreaker from making more rainy recesses?" he asked.

Melody used an eyedropper to add four drops of a pasty blue liquid to her cupcake batter. "Maybe I like rainy recesses," she told her brother. "Maybe I like that you have to sit next to Myrna Breckstein in the library."

Horace gazed down into the bowl of batter.

It looked like a mixture of fingernails, chewed bubblegum, and barbecue sauce. "You're just mad that I didn't come home with you," he told his sister. "You can't boss me around all the time. Xax, Auggie, and I were busy trying to figure out who the Heartbreaker is."

Melody chopped up a dozen pigeon feathers and sprinkled them into the mixture. "If you want to solve this with your friends, go right ahead, but the Cupcaked Crusader is *my* superhero, and I think he could put a stop to the Heartbreaker better than the Blootin Twins and Shortcake Splattly."

Horace fumed.

Shortcake Splattly!

Melody's superhero!

Without superpowered cupcakes, Melody thinks I'm nothing!

Horace stomped a foot to the ground, grabbed Melody's bowl out of her hands, and flung it across her bedroom. The mixing bowl flew out the window. Horace could hear it thump against the ground below. "I am *not* Shortcake Splatly. I'm not nothing without you! I'm the Cupcaked Crusader!" he yelled at his sister. "I have a plan to catch the Heartbreaker, and I'm going to do it with or without your cupcakes!"

Melody glared at her brother and leaned out her bedroom window. "That was my special batter! I've been working on it all afternoon!" she screamed.

Horace looked out the window and saw where the batter had splattered in a mess across the lawn. He shrugged. "I don't care. Now, are you going to give me cupcakes or not?" he asked.

Melody sat at her desk in front of her lavender Lily Deaver laptop computer. "Not," she replied.

A knock was heard and Dr. Splatly peeked his head in the bedroom. "Hey, what's all the yelling about?" he asked. "Why are mixing bowls flying out the window? I'm trying to help patients in my office, and you two are causing quite a ruckus."

Horace sat on Melody's bed. "Uh, sorry, Dad. Melody and I were just working on something together and—"

Melody pointed at Horace. "We were not working on something together," she said. "Horace came in here and ruined one of my science projects for no reason."

The kids' dad looked from Melody to Horace. "Did you throw that bowl out the window and ruin Melody's science project?" he asked.

Horace chewed on his lip. He didn't know how to explain to his dad what was happening with the Heartbreaker. "I did throw the bowl, but it was because she was being mean. She called me Shortcake Splattly," he said.

Dr. Splattly shook his head. "I have a patient coming in a few minutes, and I don't want to hear another yell or see another bowl fly out a window." He held the door open. "Obviously you two aren't getting along this afternoon. Horace, maybe you should play in your room and leave your sister alone."

Horace stood and looked at his dad. "But I need Melody to help me with something," he said.

Melody stood and looked at her dad. "I don't want to help him with anything ever again," she said.

Dr. Splattly looked at his watch. "I don't have time for this now. We'll discuss it after dinner. Horace, for the rest of the afternoon you are to stay in your room and Melody is to stay in her room."

Horace frowned as his father marched him into his room, then went downstairs. Horace shut the door and leaned his back against it. There had to be some way to get cupcakes from his sister so he could have powers.

And then he remembered what Melody had told him when he'd saved her from the raging river. She'd said that if he saved her, she promised to share her secret stash of cupcakes with him!

Horace opened his closet door, pushed his way between the hanging clothes, and cupped his hands against the back wall. On the other side of the closet wall was Melody's desk in her room. "Hey!" he called. "You promised me that if I swung you over the river, you'd share your secret stash of cupcakes, so now you have to give me some!"

Horace pressed his ear to the wall.

"I don't have to share anything with you, because you don't listen to me," Melody said back through the wall.

Horace cupped his hands against the wall again. "Well, if you don't share the cupcake stash, then I'm going to join up with the Heartbreaker. She said that if I team up with her, she can make me even more powerful and we can take over the school together. Do you really want to lose *your* superhero to the enemy?" he asked.

Horace pressed his ear to the wall and listened for Melody's response.

Swoooooooooosh!

A panel of the closet wall slid open to reveal a glass vault between Horace and Melody's bedrooms. It was about the size of a small freezer and had four shelves filled with all different kinds of cupcakes. One was green and stood on four small table legs like it was a piece of doll furniture, another looked like a stapler with flowers growing out of it, and a third was in the shape of a duck's head with antennae on top. There must have been at least thirty cupcakes inside the glass! Each cupcake was sealed in a clear baggie and had a label with strange scribbles on it.

Horace couldn't believe his sister had so many cupcakes stored away and ready to use. He'd always thought she made them one or two at a time and then gave them to him. He'd never known she had a supply hidden away in a secret vault.

Horace looked through the glass freezer to the angry face of his sister on the other side. He held up a hand and waved to her. "So what do you think?" he asked.

Through the glass, Melody stared at her brother, her face red with fury. "The Cupcaked Crusader isn't working with anyone but me," she said. "So don't even think about it."

• • •

Melody handed Horace two of the cupcakes. "What are you using them for? Tell me," she ordered.

Horace stood beside Melody in her room and looked at the baggies. The cupcakes inside were frozen solid. The labels had strange letters and numbers written on them. "What do the symbols mean?" he asked.

Melody closed the door of her freezer vault and pushed a button, sealing the wall so it looked normal again. "Those are just my code so I know when I made them and what their ingredients are," she answered. "Nothing you need to worry about." She turned and faced her brother. "So what are you up to?"

Horace took the cupcake bags and tucked them under an arm. "Auggie and Xax are planning to try and catch the Heartbreaker on their own. They said they want to be superheroes like the Cupcaked Crusader. I told them not to do it, but they wouldn't listen," he said. Just because Melody agreed to share the cupcakes didn't mean that Horace had to tell her everything.

"So, why do you need the cupcakes?" his sister asked.

"I'm going to hide and watch what happens. If they get into trouble, I'll become the Cupcaked Crusader and help," Horace said.

Melody sat at her desk and picked up a piece of construction paper. "That seems silly to me, but okay," she said. She wrote some notes on a piece of paper. "Here are some instructions on how to eat the cupcakes." She held the piece of paper out to Horace.

Horace remembered the piece of paper Melody invented that jumped on his face. "Uh, are you sure that's safe for me to take?" he asked.

Melody folded the paper and tucked it in

her brother's pant pocket. "I programmed the paper so it belongs to you," she told him. "If you need to eat the cupcakes, read the instructions on the note first."

Horace carried the two frozen cupcakes out of Melody's room and went back to his bedroom. Why did he need instructions on how to eat cupcakes?

Ridiculous.

OFF WITH HIS HEAD

At the edge of Blootinville, high in Rumbly Mountain, the Happy Dead Man River met up with the Unhappy Dead Man River. The two rivers combined to make one river called the Happy-but-Sort-of-Unhappy Dead Man River. This massive river spilled over a cliff into Lake Honkaninny five hundred feet below.

This was Crawlyworm Falls.

Crawlyworm Falls was named after the crawlyworm. Every night, thousands of the giant, orange, glow-in-the-dark worms crawled up the falls and lay across the top, blocking the river from spilling into the gorge. As the crawly-worms blocked the river, they inflated to become large crawlyworm inner tubes. Once fully inflated, the crawlyworms break their dam and float over the falls, shouting with wormy glee as they splashed into the gorge below.

The weather tower stood in the center of the river above Crawlyworm Falls. The steel tower rose fifty feet in the air, with a large satellite dish spinning at the top. A ladder led up from the base of the tower to its top, hundreds of feet over the river.

The time was 11:58 P.M., two minutes before midnight. Horace, Xax, and Auggie lay low in the bushes by the river's edge, listening to the roar of the water as it crashed over the cliff and into the gorge. Horace was in his Cupcaked Crusader costume. The two cupcakes and Melody's note were zipped in his wing pocket. Auggie was disguised as a bush with leafy arms and legs. Xax was disguised as a large, orange crawlyworm. He even had a switch inside his costume that could light him up to glow in the dark.

Floating on a raft in front of the boys was the fake Cupcaked Crusader. Xax and Auggie had made a fake Cupcaked Crusader costume out of one of their mother's old dresses then stuffed it full of crumpled newspaper. They attached a speaker inside the dummy's mouth. Horace held a remote-control microphone in his hand.

"Are you sure this will work?" he asked.

"Try it out," Auggie said. "Just push the button on the remote and talk into the speaker."

Horace did as Auggie had said. "Testing-testing-testing," he said in his Cupcaked Crusader voice.

"Testing-testing-testing," the speaker in the dummy's mouth said in Horace's voice.

Horace grinned. "It's perfect. In the dark, the Heartbreaker will never know the dummy's not me."

Auggie looked at his watch. "We don't have any time to waste. We have to push the raft over to the weather tower so the Heartbreaker sees the dummy when she gets here."

Xax put his hands on the raft. "Ready to launch?" he asked.

Horace and Auggie put their hands on it, too. "Ready," both boys said.

"Great," Xax said. "I'll start counting. When I get to thirty-one, we'll all shove the raft to the center of the river so it can dock at the bottom of the weather tower."

Horace looked at Xax. "Do you have to count to thirty-one?" he asked. "Can't you just count to three?"

"Thirty-one is my good-luck number," Xax said.

"Then count fast," Auggie said.

"Okay, okay," Xax said. "One—two—three—four—five—six—seven—eight—nine—ten—eleven—twelve—thirteen—fourteen—fifteen—sixteen—seventeen—eighteen—nineteen—

twenty—twenty-one—twenty-two—twenty-three—twenty-four—twenty-five—twenty-six—twenty-seven—twenty-eight—twenty-nine—thirty—thirty-one . . . *Push!*"

The three boys pushed as hard as they could, sailing the raft into the water. For a second it looked like it might float down the river and over Crawlyworm Falls, but a strong breeze caught the raft and docked it right against the weather tower. It got stuck between two of the tower's large steel legs, just as the boys had planned.

"Perfect," Auggie whispered.

"See? I told you the number thirty-one was lucky," Xax said.

"Shhhh—look," Horace said. He pointed to the sky. Flying through the air was the Heartbreaker. She wore her flying jetpack and landed at the top of the weather tower. She flicked on a high-beam flashlight and waved it at the river and Crawlyworm Falls.

The three boys ducked deep in the bushes

just in case she waved the flashlight in their direction.

"Cupcaked Crusader, are you here?" the Heartbreaker asked.

"Talk into the microphone," Auggie said.

Horace pushed the button and spoke in his Cupcaked Crusader voice. *"Yes, I'm down here,"* he said, and his voice came out of the dummy Cupcaked Crusader's head on the raft at the bottom of the weather tower.

The Heartbreaker shone her flashlight down on the dummy Cupcaked Crusader. "What are you doing way down there? Climb up the ladder and meet me. It's much nicer at the top of the tower," she said.

Horace looked to Auggie and Xax. "What do I say?" he whispered.

"Tell her you're afraid of heights," Xax said.

"Tell her you broke your legs and arms, so you can't climb the ladder," Auggie said.

Horace pushed the microphone's button and spoke. *"Uh, I like it down here,"* he said. *"Uh, the way the moonlight sparkles on the water reminds me of your sparkly eyes. I think it's very romantic.*"

The Heartbreaker smiled down at the dummy Cupcaked Crusader. "That's so sweet!" she said. "Climb up the ladder and you can see my sparkly eyes up close."

"*Uh, no thanks. I think I'll stay down here,*" Horace said.

The Heartbreaker sat in the satellite dish and crossed her legs. "Do you want me to make you come up here?" she asked.

"*No no, please don't,*" Horace said. "*I'm very shy and think we shouldn't get close yet.*"

The Heartbreaker frowned and took a small metal box from a pocket of her jetpack. "I don't take no for an answer. Don't you understand that?" she asked. She pushed a button on the box and a large hook popped out on a chain that dropped down to the Cupcaked Crusader dummy.

"*Hey, don't do that!*" Horace yelled into the microphone.

The hook grabbed the Cupcaked Crusader dummy in the back of the neck.

"If you won't climb up to me, I'll just have to carry you up," the Heartbreaker said. She pushed another button on the box and the chain reversed, yanking the dummy off the raft.

As the chain lifted the dummy into the air, the hook dug so deep into its neck that the dummy's head tore off. The hook lifted the dummy's head higher in the air while the body splashed into the river and floated over the falls.

"What have I done?!" the Heartbreaker screamed. "I only wanted us to be boyfriend and girlfriend and now I've ruined everything!"

"What do we do?" Horace whispered to the twins.

"Maybe she'll get scared and fly away," Auggie said.

"Maybe she'll take off her mask and cry," Xax said.

The hook carried the dummy's head to the top of the weather tower. The Heartbreaker shone her flashlight on it, reached inside its

neck, and pulled out a piece of newspaper.

"Ouch, that hurts!" Horace said. *"Leave my head alone!"*

"Did you really think you could fool me?" the Heartbreaker screamed. She reached inside the dummy's head, yanked out the speaker, then tossed both the head and speaker down to the river below. "Nobody breaks the Heartbreaker's heart! Whoever did this is going to be *very* sorry *very* soon!" She blasted off the weather tower and flew down by the falls, shining her flashlight along the riverbank.

The boys cowered deep in the bushes.

"What'll we do?" Auggie asked.

"Just lay quiet, so she won't hear us," Horace said.

"I think my crawlyworm costume is stuck on a branch," Xax said. He wriggled back and forth, creating a stir in the bushes. Suddenly his costume lit up a bright glow-in-the dark orange.

"What are you doing?" Horace asked. He rolled away from Xax so he wouldn't get caught in the light of the glowing worm costume.

"Turn that off," Auggie hissed, moving away from his brother.

"I can't. The switch broke," Xax said.

A bright flashlight beamed on Xax's crawlyworm head. "Well, look what I've found," the Heartbreaker said. "Only the Cupcaked Crusader knew I was coming here tonight, so he must have teamed up with someone to try and catch me. That must mean he's somewhere around here, too."

Xax tried to wriggle behind a bush. "You won't get me, or him. We have a plan and we're going to stop you," he said.

The Heartbreaker flew right above Xax. "A plan? Is that right?" she asked. "We'll see about that." She pressed a button on her control box, and a metal claw came out and grabbed the back of Xax's crawlyworm costume. The Heartbreaker flew high in the air, dangling Xax from the claw so he hung right over Crawlyworm Falls. "If the Cupcaked Crusader wants to keep you alive, he'd better come out and face me," the Heartbreaker said.

"Helphelphelphelphelphelphelphelphelphelp helphelphelphelphelphelphelphelphelphelphelp helphelphelphelphelphelphelphelphelphelp," Xax called.

Auggie tugged on Horace's cape. "You've got to do something to save Xax," he said. "You've got to."

"I know, I know," Horace said. He quickly

reached inside his cape and took out the two cupcakes and the note with Melody's instructions.

"Hurry and eat them," Auggie said.

The Heartbreaker dangled Xax lower to the river. He looked like a giant orange glowing worm flying through the night sky. "Come out, Cupcaked Crusader or your friend will be swimming with the crawlyworms forever!" the Heartbreaker taunted.

Horace tried to read Melody's note, but it was too dark, so he shoved it back in his cape pocket. He took the two cupcakes out of their baggies. Because he couldn't see them in the dark, he could only feel what they were like. One was furry and felt like an animal. The other felt mushy, like wet noodles with cold glop on top.

"Hurry up, Cupcaked Crusader," the Heartbreaker called.

"I'll be there in a second," Horace yelled in his Cupcaked Crusader voice. Without another thought, he popped the furry cupcake into his mouth and chewed. It tasted like he was licking a dog that had rolled in dirt. He swallowed it, then stuck the entire noodle cupcake in his mouth. This one tasted like cold spaghetti with tomato sauce. He chewed it fast and swallowed, waiting for something to happen.

The Cupcaked Crusader didn't have long to wait. Seconds later, his body began changing.

SHOWDOWN OVER CRAWLYWORM FALLS

"Horace, what's going on?" Auggie asked, waving an arm of his bush costume in his friend's face. "Are you ready to save Xax?"

Horace didn't answer. He was too busy thinking about what was happening in his body. He felt a strange thing pushing at the inside of his lower back, like it was trying to get out. It pushed harder and harder until he felt something burst out his back and through his Cupcaked Crusader costume. He reached back a hand and felt it. It was furry and kept growing until it was about twenty feet long.

Horace had grown a gigantic tail!

But before he could get used to that, two other strange things happened. His fingernails grew longer and cut through the gloves of both arms of the costume. The fingernails of one hand began dripping gobs of tomato sauce. The fingernails of his other hand began growing strands of hot spaghetti. When he pointed his fingers, one hand sprayed tomato sauce like a high-powered water gun, and the other hand shot out a rope of spaghetti.

The Cupcaked Crusader had become a pasta machine!

Auggie shook Horace's shoulder. "Is everything okay?" he asked.

Horace turned to his friend. "Don't worry, Xax will be fine," he said. The Cupcaked Crusader leaped out of the bushes and stood on the riverbank. He whipped his tail across the river, grabbed hold of the weather tower, and swung himself over to it. "Hey, Heartbreaker, look who's here?!" he teased.

The Heartbreaker shone her flashlight on the Cupcaked Crusader. "So you've finally shown yourself," she said. She flew closer to Horace, landing beside him on the weather tower. Xax dangled from the claw attached to her control box.

Horace shot long spaghetti strands out of his hand, wrapping Xax in a pasta net. "It's me you want. Let go of him and we can talk," he told the Heartbreaker.

The Heartbreaker put her lips next to Horace's ear. "If I let the kid go, will you promise to join me?" she asked.

Horace shut his eyes really tight, puckered his lips, and gave the Heartbreaker a kiss on the cheek. "Sure," he said. "No problem," he added softly. What he really wanted to do was spit and wipe his lips on the sleeve of his costume, but he knew that the Heartbreaker would get mad if he did.

The Heartbreaker blushed. "Great," she said. She pushed a button on her box and released the claw that was hanging on to Xax. Horace used his spaghetti strands to swing Xax to the riverbank.

But the spaghetti wasn't strong enough. The strands snapped, and Xax fell through the air and dropped into the river.

"Save me!" Xax called from inside his glowing orange crawlyworm costume.

"Do something!" Auggie yelled.

Horace didn't know what to do! He was hanging from the tower with his tail, and his spaghetti and sauce powers weren't strong enough to hold Xax. His friend was floating down the river, heading straight for the falls.

Just as Xax was about to spill over and drop five hundred feet into the gorge, thousands and thousands of giant orange glow-in-the-dark crawlyworms appeared at the top of the waterfall. The crawlyworms formed a huge dam, blocking the river from flowing over the cliff.

Xax floated up against the crawlyworm dam and stayed there. Then the crawlyworms slowly curled and inflated, getting fatter and fatter like inner tubes.

"Get me out of here before the crawlyworms drop over the falls and the river starts again," Xax called.

Horace looked the Heartbreaker in the eyes. "Miss Heartbreaker, can you please use your claw to lift him to land," he said, pretending to like her. "Then we can have a dinner date on the top of the weather tower."

"Deal," the Heartbreaker said. She pushed a button on her metal box, and the claw sprang out, grabbed Xax, and carried him out of the river and dropped him onto the riverbank.

By now, the crawlyworms had inflated to full inner tubes. They broke their dam and spilled over the falls, cheering with wormy glee. The river began flowing over the cliff with a giant wave of water.

Xax stood at the side of the river in his costume. "That's the last time I ever become a crawlyworm," he said.

Auggie tugged on Xax's costume, pulling his brother into the bushes. "Get back here and hide," he said.

The Heartbreaker wasn't paying attention to the twins. She was staring at the Cupcaked Crusader. "I think it's time for our date," she said. She flew to the top of the weather tower and sat in the satellite dish, waving down to the Cupcaked Crusader. "Ready to join me?" she asked.

Horace wasn't sure he wanted to have a date with the Heartbreaker, but he knew it might be the only way to find out who she was. He flicked his giant tail and wrapped it around the top of the tower, then he climbed up it. He sat in the satellite dish face-to-face with his enemy.

"Shall we dine?" the Heartbreaker asked.

Horace wasn't sure what to do. Should they eat together so he could get her mask off, or would she try to trap him? He held out his hands and blasted a pile of spaghetti and sauce onto the satellite dish. "Uh, I'm not sure how we can eat without forks," he said.

The Heartbreaker giggled and covered her mouth with a hand. "Oh, I can take care of that," she said. The villain clicked two fasteners on her control box and popped it open to show a lunch-box compartment holding forks, spoons, knives, and napkins. She handed Horace a fork and napkin and took one of each out for herself. "Eat up," she said.

Horace couldn't take his eyes off the control-box/lunch box. It was large and gray and had big steel bolts sticking out from its side. He knew he'd seen that lunch box before.

"Is that how you made the rainy recesses happen?" Horace asked. "How does it work?"

The Heartbreaker proudly displayed the lunch box, holding it up for Horace to see. It had a miniature computer screen in the inside of the top lid and all sorts of buttons and a keyboard in the bottom, with an empty space for a thermos and lunch. "All I have to do is enter the longitude, latitude, and square footage of the area I want it to rain on. Then the lunch box emits radioactive waves that increase the humidity over the area until a cloud forms and the rain pours down. I can even set it on a timer for however long I want it to rain," the Heartbreaker said with a smile. "It's really quite simple."

Horace watched lights blink on and off across the computer screen. It had a picture of Blootinville on it with a blinking star in the center at Crawlyworm Falls. "It looks pretty complicated to me," he told the Heartbreaker. "How'd you get to be so smart to make it and your jetpack? You must be a genius."

The Heartbreaker blushed, and swatted Horace playfully with a hand. "Oh, how you flatter me, Cupcaked Crusader," she said. "Let's just say that when you don't have many friends, you have a lot of time to read and figure things out. That's how I learned to invent things. And I'm lucky enough to be very closely related to people who can give me lots of information about weather or anything else I want to know." She put the lunch box beside her. "But I don't want to discuss work. This is supposed to be a date."

The Heartbreaker took her fork, twirled spaghetti on it, and took a bite. "Scrumptious! You make delicious spaghetti," she said, giving Horace a wink. "I like a superhero who can cook."

Horace put down his fork and napkin. "Well, I'm a good guy. I wish you wouldn't use your smarts to make rainy recesses or dangle my friends over waterfalls," he told the Heart-breaker.

The Heartbreaker blinked her eyes and laid down her fork. "Oh, I never would have hurt your friend. I just wanted to get you to team up with me," she explained, taking Horace's hands in her own. "And the rainy recesses didn't hurt anyone. I just did those so I could sit in the library with a boy I liked." A small tear ran out of the Heartbreaker's eye. "Really, I never ever meant to hurt anyone. I just wanted him to like me."

Horace stared at the girl in the black suit with the red heart. He didn't need to take off her mask to know who she was. She was just a girl he had talked to before. A girl who had stood on the playground swinging a large steel lunch box against the side of the school.

She'd gotten all her book smarts from her mother: Librarian Breckstein.

She'd gotten all her weather smarts from her father: Weatherman Breckstein.

The Heartbreaker was Myrna Breckstein.

"Don't you want to be on my team?" the girl asked, squeezing Horace's hands. "If I had a boyfriend like you, I wouldn't need to make any more rainy recesses to sit with that other boy. You're much more interesting and smarter and cuter than he is."

Horace stood up on the satellite dish. "I think you should put away your machines and stop trying to force people to be your friends. Maybe if you were just nice to kids, they would be friends with you, and you wouldn't have to make it rain at recess or dangle kids over waterfalls," he said.

The Heartbreaker stood up, too. "I don't want *friends*, Cupcaked Crusader. I don't need friends. I just want a *boyfriend*, so we can be powerful together and rule the world. Is there anything wrong with that?" She picked up her lunch box. "Now, are you going to be on my team or not?" she asked, her voice growing louder. She reached down to push some buttons on the control panel.

Horace looked deep into the eyes of the Heartbreaker. She was the most evil, friendly villain he'd ever met. She was smart and sweet and nasty all at the same time. If she wasn't so bad, she could probably be a good girlfriend.

If Horace wanted a girlfriend. Which he didn't.

The wind blew Horace's cape in the air behind him. He curled his hands into fists and pressed them to his hips. "I don't want anything to do with you," he told the Heartbreaker. "You're too evil for me."

The Heartbreaker gasped and stomped her foot on the satellite dish. "You have to be on my team! You have to!" she commanded.

"It's not going to happen," the Cupcaked Crusader told her.

The Heartbreaker typed into the keyboard in her lunch box, and a storm cloud suddenly appeared above their heads. "Change your mind," she said.

"No way," Horace said.

The Heartbreaker pushed another button. Lightning bolts burst from the cloud and shot down all around Horace.

"Did you really think I'd take no for an answer?" the Heartbreaker asked.

More lightning bolts crashed down around Horace, trapping him on the weather tower.

The Heartbreaker reached a hand out to pull off the Cupcaked Crusader's mask. "Now it's time to find out who you really are," she said.

But before she could grab it, Horace took Melody's special construction-paper note out of his wing pocket. "Wait! This note will tell you who I am," he said, holding out the piece of paper.

Thunder boomed. Lightning flashed and crashed.

"Give it to me," the Heartbreaker ordered, snatching the piece of paper from Horace's hand. The instant she grabbed the note, the paper jumped on her face, wrapping around her head. The alarm went off, blasting into the villain's ears.

"What have you done?! Get this off me!" the Heartbreaker cried, putting her hands to her paper-covered face and dropping the lunch box. The steel box fell against the tower, smashing into bits and pieces before dropping into the river below.

The storm cloud vanished, and the lightning and thunder stopped.

"You made me lose my lunch box!" the Heartbreaker cried, tearing at the construction paper that covered her face. "Get this off me!"

"Get it off yourself," Horace said. He flung his long tail across to a bush, swung down from the weather tower, and landed by the river.

"I'll get you yet, Cupcaked Crusader!" the Heartbreaker yelled. "I'll make you like me! Just you wait!"

Xax and Auggie ran to Horace.

"Why is she screaming?" Auggie asked.

"What's all that noise?" Xax asked.

Horace started running, leading the boys away from Crawlyworm Falls to where they'd parked their bikes. "That's the sound of an unhappy villain with one of Melody's inventions stuck to her face," he said. He wrapped his tail around his waist and hopped on his bike. "And I think we better get out of here before she can get it off."

THE BEST RECESS EVER

The Blootinville Elementary School lunchroom was packed with kids. All of them were eating their lunch and looking out the windows.

The sky above the playground was bright blue. There wasn't a cloud to be seen for miles.

At least not yet.

"Do you think it will rain today?" Xax asked.

"Are you sure the Heartbreaker won't ruin it?" Auggie asked.

Horace looked across the room at Myrna.

She sat at a lunch table with a new regular-size lunch box. It didn't look like it had any special controls or powers. Sitting at the table with her was Melody and Melody's best friend, Betsy Roach. Myrna was smiling and laughing with the girls. "I'm pretty sure it's not going to rain at this recess," he said.

By the time Horace had arrived home from Crawlyworm Falls the previous night, his powers were gone, and he'd slipped under his bedcovers and gotten a good night's sleep. That morning at breakfast, he told Melody that he'd make sure it wouldn't rain at recess if she would do him one small favor and try to be friends with Myrna Breckstein at lunch and recess.

Melody laughed at her brother. "You just don't want her telling everyone that you're her boyfriend," she said.

Horace laughed, too. "That's right. I don't. But I also think she's pretty smart and that you might like her," he said.

Melody looked at her brother. "Okay, but if I

do it, there's one more thing you have to do for me," she said. "After school, you have to wash all my lavender Lily Deaver underwear in the bathtub, then iron and fold it, and put it away in my dresser."

The idea of washing Melody's underwear was one of the worst things Horace could think of doing, but that was probably better than all the kids at school thinking he was going to marry Myrna Breckstein. Horace didn't want Myrna to be lonely or be the Cupcaked Crusader's enemy, but he didn't want to marry her either. "Okay, I'll do it," he told his sister, finishing up his cereal bowl of Celernos.

In the lunchroom, Myrna walked over to Horace and draped her arms around his neck. "Hiya, my mini-hunk. Guess what?" she asked.

Horace dipped his head out of the loop Myrna's arms made. He looked over at his sister. She was supposed to be making friends with Myrna so she'd stay away from him. "Uh, what is it, Myrna?" he asked.

Myrna giggled. "I know why you want Melody to be my friend," she said. "After you and I are married, she's going to be my sister-in-law! I can hardly wait! Melody even said she'd help me plan the wedding! Isn't that the best?" Myrna kissed Horace's cheek and ran back to her lunch table.

Xax and Auggie laughed hysterically.

"You're going to marry Myrna!" Auggie teased.

"Where are you going to go on your honeymoon?" Xax asked. "Storybook Land or Old MacDonald's Farm?"

Horace gritted his teeth and shook his head. "That's not going to happen. No way. No how," he told his friends.

At that moment Principal Nosair stood in front of all the kids and clapped his hands. "Okay, everyone, since it's not raining, you can head out onto the playground!" he announced.

Mr. Dienow swung the door to the playground open. "Get out of here and leave me alone!" he yelled.

"Hooray!" the kids cheered. They tossed their

lunch trash away and ran out the cafeteria doors to the Esophagus Eliminator. Other kids played Blootinville Ball and Celernip Toss.

Horace, Auggie, and Xax strolled out of the cafeteria and stood by the side of the school.

The twins looked up at the sky.

"No clouds at all," Auggie said. "Not one."

"I can't believe you didn't find out who the Heartbreaker really is," Xax said.

Horace hadn't told his friends or Melody that he'd found out who the Heartbreaker really was. He didn't want to get Myrna in trouble. The most important thing was to keep her from doing any more damage, and Horace thought he'd stopped her. At least for now. He still remembered the last thing the Heartbreaker had said to him on the weather tower. She'd told him that she'd make the Cupcaked Crusader a part of her team.

Could she make that happen? Would the Heartbreaker come back and do something to try to get him to join forces with her?

Myrna, Melody, and Betsy climbed on the

Twisted Maniac, getting their arms and legs tangled in one another's. The three girls were smiling and laughing. Maybe Melody would like Myrna so much that Melody wouldn't make him wash her underwear that afternoon, Horace thought.

Maybe, but probably not. Melody loved watching her brother do stupid things, and since Horace had already said he would do her laundry, she was sure to make him. Plus now she was also going to help plan Myrna's wedding!

Maybe having Melody and Myrna be friends wasn't such a good idea after all.

The three boys walked across the playground and sat under a tree. Xax reached into his backpack and pulled out *The Splattly & Blootin Big Book of Worldwide Conspiracies*.

Auggie took the notebook and folded it open to the page on "The Investigation of the Rainy Recesses."

"Do you think the Heartbreaker will come back?" Xax asked.

Horace thought long and hard, then longer and harder. "I don't know," he told his friends. "She said she would, but maybe she won't. We'll just have to wait and see."

Auggie took the cap off a marker. "What should I write at the bottom of the page?" he asked.

Xax sat up. "Write that that Heartbreaker almost dropped me over the edge of the waterfall," he said.

Auggie began to write, but Horace took his hand and stopped him. "No, don't write that. That was kind of my fault when the spaghetti strands broke," he said.

"That is kind of true," Xax said.

Auggie looked at Horace. "Then what should I write?" he asked.

"Look up at the sky," Horace told his friends. "Just write that 'The Investigation of the Rainy Recesses' is over, then let's just go play on the Esophagus Eliminator."

Xax smiled. "That sounds like a good idea to me," he said.

"Case closed, it is," Auggie said, and he began writing in the book.

Horace shook his head and looked across the playground at Myrna Breckstein playing. It was good that the Cupcaked Crusader had stopped the Heartbreaker from making rainy recesses, but still, Horace had one other problem . . .

How in the world was he going to stop Myrna from marrying him?